Published by Ladybird Books Ltd
A Penguin Company
Penguin Books Ltd, 80 Strand, London WC2R 0RL, UK
Penguin Books Australia Ltd, Camberwell, Victoria, Australia
Penguin Books (NZ) Ltd, Cnr Airbourne and Rosedale Roads, Albany, Auckland, 1310, New Zealand

1 3 5 7 9 10 8 6 4 2

© LADYBIRD BOOKS MMV

1844226824

9781844226825

Printed in Italy

FAVOURITE TALES

The Tortoise Who Wanted to Fly

Retold by Lorraine Horsley
Illustrated by Maggy Roberts

Long ago, when the world was young, Tortoise's shell wasn't cracked and ugly as it is now. It was smooth and shiny and shone like a pebble in the sunlight.

All the birds of the world loved Tortoise's shell. They polished it with their wings until it was so smooth they could see their reflections in it. Then they would sit fluffing their feathers to make sure every one was in place.

As the birds primped and preened,
Tortoise gazed in wonder at their
beautiful feathers. How he longed to
have feathers of his own to lift him
up into the sky! For, more than anything
in the world, Tortoise wanted to fly.

Then, one day, Eagle came to call. "I'm
having a party for all the birds," he told
Tortoise. "Would you like to come?"

Tortoise was overjoyed. "Yes, please!"
he cried.

"Good," replied Eagle. "The party starts
at twelve o'clock at my house." And with
that, Eagle flapped his mighty wings and
flew out of sight.

Tortoise began to cry. "Eagle lives at the top of the highest mountain!" he sobbed. "How will I get there? It's too far to climb. Oh, if only I could fly!"

In a nearby tree sat Dove. She saw how upset Tortoise was and wanted to help him. She fluttered down from her branch and hopped up to Tortoise.

"Cheer up," said Dove. "I have a plan. Wait here and I'll see what I can do."

The next day, Tortoise was woken by the sound of a thousand birds chirruping and cheeping. He poked his head out of his shell to see what was happening.

"Good morning, Tortoise," said Dove. "We have come to help you to fly. All you need are some feathers!"

And one by one the birds stepped forward to pluck out their finest feather and place it on the ground at Tortoise's feet.

"Now we must stick them to your shell,"
said Hummingbird.

Swallow collected some sticky mud and
Flamingo used it to glue the feathers all
over Tortoise's shell. Before long, Tortoise
was completely covered in feathers of
every shape and size. Two long wings
stretched out at his sides.

"You look wonderful," said Kingbird.
"Now come with us to Eagle's home in
the clouds."

Tortoise flapped his new wings and slowly, slowly, rose off the ground.

"At last!" he cried. "I can fly!"

Very soon, Tortoise was swooping in and out of the trees, skimming over the waves and soaring above the clouds.

"This is even better than I dreamed it would be," thought Tortoise.

At last Tortoise reached the mountain where Eagle lived. The birds were already there, waiting for Tortoise to arrive.

"Welcome!" said Eagle. He was pleased to see his friend, but he was surprised that Tortoise had feathers of his own.

Eagle turned to the birds and smiled. "Thank you for coming," he said. "I have prepared a wonderful feast for you all."

Tortoise and the birds followed Eagle to a
table covered with delicious food of every
kind. There were steaming plates of yams
and rice, ripe mangoes and large juicy
melons. There were rainbow fish and
crab dumplings and sweet honey cakes.

Tortoise couldn't believe his eyes.

Tortoise was hungry after his long journey. Forgetting his manners, he rushed to the table, scattering the birds in all directions and trampling poor Dove beneath his feet.

The birds watched in horror as their
friend grabbed all the food and
gobbled it down. Soon, there was
nothing left but crumbs.

The birds were angry with Tortoise for eating all the delicious food, so they pulled and tugged at the feathers on his shell until there were none left. Then they rolled him to the edge of the mountain and pushed him off.

Crash! Smack! Tortoise tumbled down the mountain, bouncing off rocks and slipping over stones as he went. By the time he reached the bottom, his beautiful shell was scratched and dirty and covered in cracks.

Tortoise stumbled to his feet, dazed and bruised. "I never, EVER, want to fly again," he groaned.

And to this day, Tortoise creeps slowly
around, taking great care with his
cracked shell, just in case it breaks.